MAY 2013

P9-CSW-347

This book belongs to

_____

Franklin in the Dark

25th Anniversary Edition

To Natalie and Gordon — P.B.

For Bob and Robin, with love — B.C.

Franklin

Franklin is a trademark of Kids Can Press Ltd.

Franklin in the Dark originally published in 1986
Franklin in the Dark: 25th Anniversary Edition published in 2011

Text © Contextx Inc. 1986 and 2011
Illustrations and letter on page 9 © Brenda Clark Illustrator Inc. 1986, 1991, 1994, 1995, 1996, 1997, 1998, 2000, 2002 and 2011

All rights reserved. No part of this publication may be reproduced, stored in a retrieval system or transmitted, in any form or by any means, without the prior written permission of Kids Can Press Ltd. or, in case of photocopying or other reprographic copying, a license from The Canadian Copyright Licensing Agency (Access Copyright). For an Access Copyright license, visit www.accesscopyright.ca or call toll free to 1-800-893-5777.

Kids Can Press acknowledges the financial support of the Government of Ontario, through the Ontario Media Development Corporation's Ontario Book Initiative; the Ontario Arts Council; the Canada Council for the Arts; and the Government of Canada, through the BPIDP, for our publishing activity.

Published in Canada by   Published in the U.S. by
Kids Can Press Ltd.   Kids Can Press Ltd.
25 Dockside Drive   2250 Military Road
Toronto, ON M5A 0B5   Tonawanda, NY 14150

www.kidscanpress.com

Original book edited by Ricky Englander and Valerie Hussey, designed by Michael Solomon and Brenda Clark

25th anniversary edition edited by Yvette Ghione, designed by Marie Bartholomew

CM 11 0 9 8 7 6 5 4 3 2 1

The hardcover edition of this book is smyth sewn casebound. Manufactured in Buji, Shenzhen, China, in 10/2010 by WKT Company

FSC
Mixed Sources
Product group from well-managed
forests and recycled wood or fiber
Cert no. DNV-COC-000087
www.fsc.org
©1996 Forest Stewardship Council

Photo credits

p. 7: © Laura James; **p. 9**: © David Sheffield; **pp. 46–47**: © Frank Baldassara

The images on pages 1, 2, 4–5, 8, 10 and 41 are preliminary sketches reprinted courtesy of Toronto Public Library Osborne Collection.

Library and Archives Canada Cataloguing in Publication

Bourgeois, Paulette
    Franklin in the dark / written by Paulette Bourgeois ; illustrated by Brenda Clark. — 25th anniversary ed.

ISBN 978-1-55453-616-0

1. Franklin (Fictitious character : Bourgeois) — Juvenile literature. I. Clark, Brenda II. Title.

PS8553.O85477F7 2011   jC813'.54   C2010-904761-3

Kids Can Press is a **Corus**™ Entertainment company

Franklin in the Dark

25th Anniversary Edition

Written by Paulette Bourgeois
Illustrated by Brenda Clark

Kids Can Press

Contents

The Turtle They Called Chicken

Franklin was afraid of creepy, crawly things, slippery, slimy things, monsters (dead and alive) and very high mountain ledges. Most of all he was afraid of small, dark places. And that was the real problem because ....

Franklin was a turtle. He was terrified of crawling into his small, dark shell. He was the only turtle in the whole world who dragged his shell behind him- in a wagon.

Everybody laughed at him. They pointed at him. They called him names. They yelled: "You yellow-bellied, chicken-livered, spineless excuse for a turtle." Some of them called him claustrophobic. It was terrible. He didn't even know what that meant.

Every night Franklin's mother crawled inside his shell. She looked into every corner with a flashlight.

"See," she said. "There's nothing to be afraid of."

Franklin expected his mother to say that. She wasn't afraid of anything.

Franklin couldn't stand the name-calling and all that embarrassment. He decided to leave home. He packed some bologna and mango chutney sandwiches on rye, oiled his wagon axle and headed south.

But everybody who saw Franklin the turtle laughed and laughed. They had never seen a turtle wheeling his shell behind him.

..2

The first page of Paulette's original manuscript for Franklin in the Dark

A Letter from Paulette Bourgeois

Dear Reader,

If you had told me twenty-five years ago that a little turtle named Franklin would become a family favorite all over the world, I wouldn't have believed you. Nothing that has happened to Franklin the Turtle was planned way back then.

I was a journalist when I had my first baby and I thought, naively, that since I was a writer with a child, I should start writing children's books. After hearing the television character Hawkeye on *M*A*S*H* say he was so claustrophobic that if he were a turtle, he'd be afraid of his own shell, I had my idea for a story. I wrote *Franklin in the Dark* and was thrilled when Kids Can Press decided to publish it. I was even more delighted when they asked Brenda Clark to illustrate. I thought it was a one-time deal, but readers wanted more, and so the series began.

I like to think of Franklin as just like any kid, anywhere. He and his friends share many of the same joys and sorrows, successes and failures experienced by children around the world. Franklin has been glad, sad, mad — and sometimes even bad. Many of the stories draw on my own experiences as a child (no, I wasn't afraid of the dark, but I was afraid of small spaces) and those of my two children, who grew up alongside Franklin (they both loved their blue blankets, too).

A lot of people work very hard behind the scenes to develop the best Franklin stories for the books and the animated television series, and I am very grateful that they do such a good job bringing Franklin to you. But mostly I want to thank you, the reader. Without you, there would be no reason for Franklin to celebrate his great, long adventure. Thank you for coming along.

Brenda's original storyboard for Franklin in the Dark

A Letter from Brenda Clark

Dear Reader,

There is something very special about *Franklin in the Dark*, the original Franklin story by Paulette Bourgeois. It is, without a doubt, my favorite book in the series.

Reading that first manuscript all those years ago, I felt instantly connected to Franklin's world. The images came so clearly to me that I could hardly wait to begin drawing!

My biggest challenge was designing Franklin. Because he is a turtle who acts like a boy, I wanted him to be somewhat realistic, but capable of showing human emotion. Using several different turtle references and my experience drawing children, I worked through a number of sketches before settling on Franklin's final design. He looks like a real turtle, but walks on two legs. He can crawl out of his shell and pull it behind him with a rope. Franklin is both imaginary and real.

We didn't know then that Franklin would become the star of a series of books, but Paulette had more stories to tell, and I was delighted to illustrate them. Over the years, the tales about Franklin and his friends have given me endless ideas for illustrations. For extra inspiration, I would sometimes ask my son to pose using an expression I needed for Franklin. It was also fun to add details in the art not found in the text so that readers could make their own discoveries and interact with the story. My hope is that you will enjoy returning to each book again and again.

I feel very fortunate to have spent the past twenty-five years helping to bring Franklin's stories to life. It's been an unbelievably rewarding experience. Many people have helped make Franklin a success, but I would most like to thank Kids Can Press, Paulette, my family and especially all of you who have welcomed this special little turtle into your lives.

Introducing my very first adventure …

Franklin in the Dark

Written by Paulette Bourgeois
Illustrated by Brenda Clark

Kids Can Press

FRANKLIN could slide down a riverbank all by himself. He could count forwards and backwards. He could even zip zippers and button buttons. But Franklin was afraid of small, dark places and that was a problem because …

Franklin was a turtle. He was afraid of crawling
into his small, dark shell. And so, Franklin the
turtle dragged his shell behind him.

Every night, Franklin's mother would take a
flashlight and shine it into his shell.

"See," she would say, "there's nothing to be
afraid of."

She always said that. She wasn't afraid of
anything. But Franklin was sure that creepy things,
slippery things, and monsters lived inside his
small, dark shell.

So Franklin went looking for help. He walked until he met a duck.

"Excuse me, Duck. I'm afraid of small, dark places and I can't crawl inside my shell. Can you help me?"

"Maybe," quacked the duck. "You see, I'm afraid of very deep water. Sometimes, when nobody is watching, I wear my water wings. Would my water wings help you?"

"No," said Franklin. "I'm not afraid of water."

So Franklin walked and walked until he met a lion.

"Excuse me, Lion. I'm afraid of small, dark places and I can't crawl inside my shell. Can you help me?"

"Maybe," roared the lion. "You see, I'm afraid of great, loud noises. Sometimes, when nobody is looking, I wear my earmuffs. Would my earmuffs help you?"

"No," said Franklin. "I'm not afraid of great, loud noises."

So Franklin walked and walked and walked until he met a bird.

"Excuse me, Bird. I'm afraid of small, dark places and I can't crawl inside my shell. Can you help me?"

"Maybe," chirped the bird. "I'm afraid of flying so high that I get dizzy and fall to the ground. Sometimes, when nobody is looking, I pull my parachute. Would my parachute help you?"

"No," said Franklin. "I'm not afraid of flying high and getting dizzy."

So Franklin walked and walked and walked and walked until he met a polar bear.

"Excuse me, Polar Bear. I'm afraid of small, dark places and I can't crawl inside my shell. Can you help me?"

"Maybe," growled the bear. "You see, I'm afraid of freezing on icy, cold nights. Sometimes, when nobody is looking, I wear my snowsuit to bed. Would my snowsuit help you?"

"No," said Franklin. "I'm not afraid of freezing on icy, cold nights."

Franklin was tired and hungry. He walked and walked and walked until he met his mother.

"Oh, Franklin. I was so afraid you were lost."

"You were afraid? I didn't know mothers were ever afraid," said Franklin.

"Well, did you find some help?" she asked.

"No. I met a duck who was afraid of deep
water."

"Hmmm," she said.

"Then I met a lion who was afraid of great, loud noises."

"Uh, hmmmm," she said.

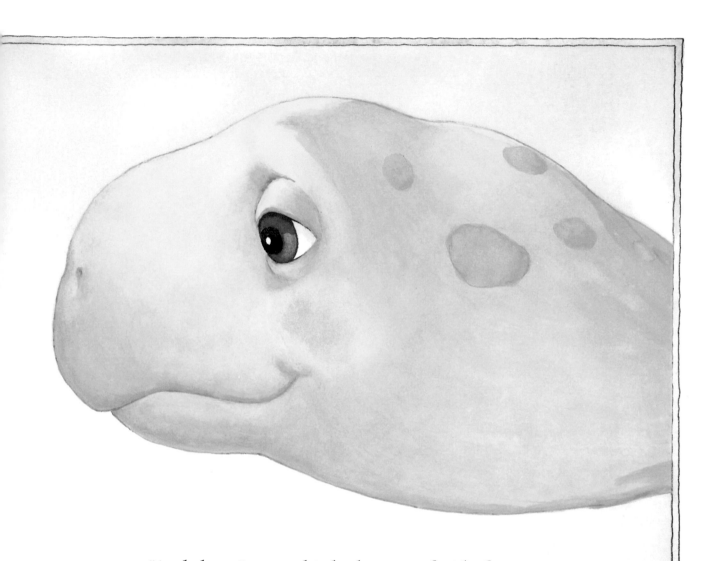

"And then I met a bird who was afraid of
falling and a polar bear who was afraid of freezing."
   "Oh," she said. "They were all afraid of
something."
   "Hmmmm," said Franklin.

It was getting late. Franklin was very tired and very hungry. They walked and walked until they were home.

Franklin's mother gave him a cold supper and a warm hug. And then she sent him off to bed. "Good night, dear," she said.

Well, Franklin knew what he had to do. He crawled right inside his small, dark shell. He was sure he saw creepy things, slippery things, and a monster. But he said a brave "Good night."

And then, when nobody was looking, Franklin the turtle turned on his night light.

Read on for the rest of the story of Franklin the Turtle …

The Story of Franklin the Turtle

In 1986, Franklin was just a little turtle trying to overcome his fear of the dark. Twenty-five years later, Franklin might still be little (and might still sleep with a night light), but he has grown into an international star!

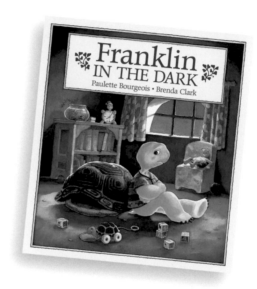

Franklin's Start

When Paulette first sent her manuscript to Kids Can Press, the title of the story was *The Turtle They Called Chicken*. In the original version, not only was Franklin afraid of the dark, he also had the problem of being teased and called "chicken." Paulette's editor suggested they focus on just one problem — Franklin's fear of the dark — and Paulette agreed. The title was changed to *Franklin in the Dark* to fit the new story. Once Paulette had finished working on the manuscript, the search for an illustrator began. Kids Can Press didn't have to look far: Brenda had already illustrated two books for them, and everyone thought her style would be perfect for Paulette's story. And it was! In its first year in print, *Franklin in the Dark* sold 10 000 copies. Children took an instant liking to the lovable turtle who experienced many of the same challenges, milestones and problems as they did.

Turtle on the Go

Delighted by readers' response to Franklin, Paulette wrote another Franklin story, and then another. Within a few years, Franklin the Turtle had become a popular book series. Franklin was busy enjoying new adventures all the time!

Learning to ride a two-wheeler.

Celebrating the holidays.

Franklin's first day of school.

Bringing Goldie home from the pet store.

Franklin's first sleepover.

The day Franklin's little sister, Harriet, was born.

Franklin's World

Together, Paulette and Brenda had created a whole world for Franklin and his family and friends. With each new book, Franklin's personality shone through more and more. Readers learned all about his favorite foods, activities and toys, and got to know the special people in his life.

Swimming at the pond

Fly pie

Sam, his stuffed dog

Painting

Mr. Owl, his teacher

Soccer

His best friend, Bear

44

Reaching for the Stars

Franklin was such a hit with readers all over the world that, by 1997, 15 million copies of the Franklin books had sold in 13 countries and in 10 different languages. That same year, Franklin made the leap to television, starring in his own animated series, which now airs throughout North America, Latin America and Europe. Franklin has also starred in two feature-length films and a stage production. More books were added to the celebrated original series, and then two new book series based on the TV show were launched, along with activity books, treasuries, flap books and other special editions.

But Franklin wasn't only found in books and on TV — Franklin-themed plush toys, puzzles, games, action figures, clothing, shoes, backpacks, lunchboxes, piggy banks, bedding, furniture and many other different products were created for the little green turtle's fans around the world.

Franklin in the Real World

Perhaps the most enduring testament to readers' love of Franklin was the opening of the Franklin Children's Garden in Toronto, Ontario, in 2003. Inspired by the original series, the garden is as special as Paulette and Brenda's books. There's a spot for storytime, a tree house, a turtle pond and even a spiral snail trail. With so much to explore, it's Franklin's world come to life!

Franklin Helps Out

Young readers' enthusiasm for Franklin is well matched by Paulette and Brenda's appreciation for his fans. In the books, although Franklin might solve his problems himself, his family, friends and neighbors all help — Franklin is part of a community. Paulette and Brenda have seen to it that Franklin plays a role in the real world's communities, too, supporting literacy campaigns, parks and wildlife societies, breakfast programs and other worthwhile causes that help make the world a better place for everyone, but especially for children.

Franklin the Turtle Today – and Tomorrow!

Now, twenty-five years after *Franklin in the Dark* was first published, over 65 million books have been sold, over 100 titles are in print and Franklin stories can be read in over thirty languages. Franklin is known as Franklin in most countries, but in French Canada he's called *Benjamin*; in Belgium and the Netherlands, *Sam*; in Finland, *Konrad*; and in Denmark, *Morten*!

A whole generation of children has grown up with Franklin, and still more adventures lie ahead: Franklin is set to star in a new animated 3D television series, more books are in development and Franklin has new community support projects on the go, too. So here's to another twenty-five years of fun and friendship – and great stories!